Dear Mrs. Cazet,
    Thank you for the work
you do in developing the self-esteem
and talents of your students.

            In friendship,
            Jeslie
            Jewis

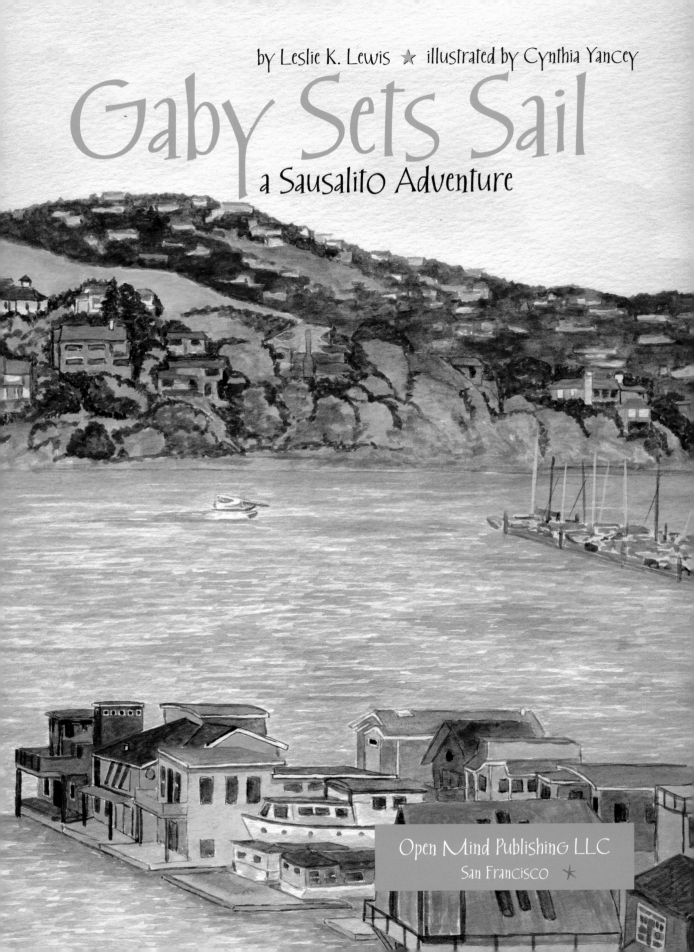

by Leslie K. Lewis ★ illustrated by Cynthia Yancey

Gaby Sets Sail
a Sausalito Adventure

Open Mind Publishing LLC
San Francisco ★

Washington, D.C., Saturday, June 6, 11:37 a.m.

My name is Gaby. I am eight years old. I am creating my first photo journal. My cat, Bella, is in most of my photos. She travels with me everywhere. Except to school. Mostly we explore our home town, Washington, D.C. It is a grand city.

Today we are taking pictures at the largest library in the world. The Library of Congress has more than 20 million books and 12 million photographs. I hope my photographs will be added to the library some day.

When I grow up, I am going to travel the world as a photo journalist. I am going to write and take pictures. Eventually, I would like to become President of the United States.

For now, Bella and I travel every summer to a new place to visit one of my aunts or uncles. We have been to New York, Chicago, and Taos, New Mexico.

Washington, D.C., Sunday, June 7, 5:00 a.m.

Bella and I wake up super early today. This morning we are flying to San Francisco. We will spend a week in Sausalito (saus/a/lito) with one of the coolest people on the planet, my Aunt Maggie. She lives on a houseboat and is a sea plane pilot.

Somewhere over Iowa, Sunday, June 7, Mid-day

We are flying in a huge plane to San Francisco. The pilot just announced that we are over Iowa. But how does he know? I see only clouds. Bella and I are reading. Aunt Maggie is going to meet us at the airport with her dog, Ace. I hope Aunt Maggie has a big car because Bella brought tons of clothes. She loves to dress up.

San Francisco Airport, Sunday, June 7, 3:00 p.m.

The plane just landed. I can see Maggie and Ace. Bella grins. She loves Ace and can't wait to help him dress with style.

At the foot of the Golden Gate Bridge, Sunday, June 7, 4:15 p.m.

Aunt Maggie takes us to see the Golden Gate Bridge. She says we should see it from under the bridge. Ace, Bella, and I crane our heads up and stare with awe at the two huge towers of the bridge. They are so tall. I almost can't see the top. Beneath the bridge, a huge freighter is passing. It looks as big as a skyscraper.

Home for a Week, Sunday, June 7, 4:41 p.m.

Sausalito is a small town just north of San Francisco. When you go across the Golden Gate Bridge, Sausalito is the first town you come to. It is right on the water. It is a great place for sailors to live. Aunt Maggie lives on the water—in a houseboat! The boat is called Bella Vita. It means "beautiful life" in Italian. To get to Aunt Maggie's boat, we must walk down a long pier lined with flowers. "Look, Bella," I shout. "The boat even has a gangplank!"

Bella Vita, Sunday, June 7, 7:15 p.m.

For dinner, Maggie cooks pasta and my favorite vegetable—artichokes! (art/i/chokes) We eat this feast outdoors—on a floating deck. A large bird sits nearby. Aunt Maggie says it is a Blue Heron. "I think he wants to be invited to dinner!" I say.

The sun sets as we finish dessert. I snap pictures of the sunset and the Blue Heron. "I could live here forever," I tell Bella. "It is so beautiful," she agrees. Before we go to bed, Maggie helps me email a few pictures to my parents and my sister, Terri.

Rowing on the Bay at Dawn, Monday, June 8

The next morning, Maggie wakes me at 5:30 a.m. "Time to greet the day," she says cheerfully. I groan but get up. Each morning Maggie rows a boat on the bay. This morning she is taking me with her.

Bella and Ace ignore us. They prefer to sleep in.

After a quick breakfast, Maggie and I put on our life vests. We are both strong swimmers, but it is best to be safe. Life vests will keep us floating if the boat flips.

Getting in the row boat is scary! "It's going to tip over!" I call out. Maggie smiles and helps me aboard. Once we are seated, the boat stops rocking. I push us away from the pier, and Maggie starts rowing. With each stroke of the oars, the boat glides forward through the water.

While Maggie rows, I take photographs. As the sun rises above the hills, pink, orange, and purple colors bounce off the clouds and water. "This is a wonderful way to greet the day," I say. Maggie just smiles. She is breathing hard now. Soon a seal joins us. He swims beside us, popping his head up every so often. It's as if he is saying, "What's taking you so long?"

Our First Boat Trip, Monday, June 8, 11:30 a.m.

In the afternoon, Maggie takes us sailing. I help raise and trim the sails. Pulling the ropes is hard work. Steering the boat is also tricky. "I have much to learn," I say over and over. Ace and Bella peek over the side, looking for whales. "There are hardly ever whales in San Francisco Bay," Maggie says. No matter. It's a great day, perfect for taking photos. I love being on the water and feeling the wind in my hair.

Caffe Trieste, Monday, June 8, 3:22 P.M.

After sailing most of the day, we head to Caffe Trieste to relax. I am excited because this restaurant is where the sailors (like me) and bicyclists (like me) hang out. We order four hot chocolates. I talk to a wise seaman named Ernie. He tells me tall tales about his sailing adventures in Alaska. As we say good bye, he says, "Gaby, you take lots of sailing lessons. There is much to learn." "I know, I known." I agree.

Biking like a Local, Tuesday, June 9, 1:49 p.m.

Today we are biking. Well, Maggie and I are biking. Bella and Ace are along for the ride. They are queen and king for the day. This morning we ride across the Golden Gate Bridge. The wind makes me shiver, but I don't mind. It is so beautiful. I am glad I have color film in my camera.

Riding down the hill to Sausalito is a thrill. I am having so much fun rowing and sailing and biking. And I feel healthier, too.

Taking the Ferry, Tuesday, June 9, 5:30 p.m.

After biking all day, we ride the ferry to San Francisco. All around us are beautiful views of the bay area. In San Francisco, we walk through China Town to get fresh produce for dinner. I'm starving. China Town is beautiful and bustling with activity.

Sailing Lessons, Wednesday, June 10, 4:52 p.m.

Today I am taking an all day sailing course. I have been here for five hours. My head is swimming with sailing terms. The teacher talks about "lines"... "jibs"... "tacks." That sailor was right. There is so much to learn.

Still, I am having fun, and I have met so many new friends. I take a picture of each one of them.

Sailing is exhausting. I will sleep well tonight.

Balancing Artists, Thursday, June 11, 11:09 a.m.

Today, we explore Sausalito. It is a charming town with lots of cafés and art galleries. When the fog clears, the sky is the brightest blue I've ever seen. I see why so many people like visiting the town.

Aunt Maggie says that "Sausalito" means "little willow" in Spanish. I know a willow is a tree, but I am not sure what it looks like. I should make a trip to the Sausalito Library and find out.

Oops! Thursday, June 11, 1:10 P.M.

That's when it happens. Bella is balancing on one paw when she loses her balance. She begins to slide down the rock. Her arms and tail swing wildly.

A second later, she drops into the bay
with a splash. "Bella!" I scream.

The crowd moves to the edge to watch Bella's struggle.

"BEL-LA!" I scream again. In full panic, I start running down to the water.

The Rescue! Thursday, June 11, 1:11 p.m.

Aunt Maggie grabs me and stops me.

Just then a sailor in a boat throws a life saver to Bella. She grabs it with her claws. She holds on for dear life.

Aunt Maggie touches my cheek. "Don't worry, honey," she says. Then she calmly walks down to the shore and wades into the water. She swims over to Bella and grabs Bella around her mid section. Aunt Maggie holds onto Bella and swims slowly back to shore.

My hero!

Aunt Maggie helps Bella out of the water.

"Oh, thank you, Aunt Maggie!" I say, hugging Bella. "You're my hero."

Then I wave to the sailor. "And thank you, too." Only then do I see that it's Ernie, the same sailor I talked to in the café.

Sailing in the FOG! Friday, June 12, 11:23 a.m.

The next morning we go sailing again. This time Bella wears two life vests. Still, she is having fun. So am I.

"Hey, somebody stole the city and Sausalito!" I say to Aunt Maggie.

Aunt Maggie smiles and says, "You think so? You don't think the fog just makes it impossible to see either San Francisco or Sausalito? I think Sausalito will come back into view as we head to shore."

Up, up and away! Friday, June 12, 2:51 p.m.

In the afternoon, Aunt Maggie takes us up in her airplane. Taxiing on the water is a thrill. As we take off and rise into the air, we pass by houses and sail boats. I grab Aunt Maggie's arm. "Hey, there's your house boat!" I take lots of pictures.

Soaring! Friday, June 12, 3:12 p.m.

Wow, San Francisco looks so small from a plane. So, does Sausalito. They remind me of the toy cities I had when I was young. After we land, we go to an art museum. There is so much to do here.

Farewell! Friday, June 12, 7:10 p.m.

That night, Aunt Maggie takes us all to dinner at Angelino's, one of her favorite restaurants. We make a toast to friendship, adventure, and following your heart's desire.

I am sad because this is our farewell dinner. Still, I miss my parents and my sister.

I thank Aunt Maggie three times for teaching me to sail and row. I think I will visit Aunt Maggie again next summer. For now, Bella and I must catch a flight home.